# I'll Be RIGHT THERE

JONATHAN MARSHALL

illustrated by Julia Ortney

ISBN: 9781699292457 (Paperback)
ISBN: 9781699292457 (Hardcover)

Front cover image by Julia Orthey
Book design by Julia Orthey

Printed by Amazon, Inc., in the United States of America.

First printing edition 2019.

Publisher: Jonathan Marshall

jmarsharts@gmail.com

This book is dedicated to Tiko & Biko.

In the middle of the **NIGHT,**

whenever you have a **FRIGHT,**

I'll be right there.

If you hear the CREAKING of a door

or a "THUMP" on the floor,

Worry no more, I'll be right there!

I could be on a boat out at SEA,

I could be climbing up a TREE,

but if you call on me...

I'll be right there!

I could be flying in a *plane*,

I could be riding on a TRAIN,

I'll be right there!

If your dreams make you **SAD**
or have you feeling **BAD**,

just yell out "Dad!"

And I'll be right there!

I know dreams sometimes are creepy,

which makes sleeping sometimes not easy,

but know if you ever need me...

I'll be right there!

Printed in Great Britain
by Amazon